THE WIFE OF BATH
AND OTHER
CANTERBURY TALES

GEOFFREY CHAUCER

THE WIFE OF BATH
AND OTHER
CANTERBURY TALES

Translated into Modern English
by Nevill Coghill

penguin books

PENGUIN BOOKS

Published by the Penguin Group
Penguin Books USA Inc., 375 Hudson Street,
New York, New York 10014, U.S.A.
Penguin Books Ltd, 27 Wrights Lane,
London W8 5TZ, England
Penguin Books Australia Ltd, Ringwood,
Victoria, Australia
Penguin Books Canada Ltd, 10 Alcorn Avenue,
Toronto, Ontario, Canada M4V 3B2
Penguin Books (N.Z.) Ltd, 182–190 Wairau Road,
Auckland 10, New Zealand

Penguin Books Ltd, Registered Offices:
Harmondsworth, Middlesex, England

Published in Penguin Books 1995

"The Wife of Bath's Tale," "The Miller's Tale," and "The Reeve's
Tale" are from Chaucer's *The Canterbury Tales*, translated by Nevill
Coghill, published by Penguin Books.

ISBN 0 14 60.0116 8

Printed in the United States of America

CONTENTS

THE WIFE OF BATH'S TALE

The Wife of Bath's Prologue

'If there were no authority on earth
Except experience, mine, for what it's worth,
And that's enough for me, all goes to show
That marriage is a misery and a woe;
For let me say, if I may make so bold,
My lords, since when I was but twelve years old,
Thanks be to God Eternal evermore,
Five husbands have I had at the church door;
Yes, it's a fact that I had so many,
All worthy in their way, as good as any.

  'Someone said recently for my persuasion
That as Christ only went on one occasion
To grace a wedding—in Cana of Galilee—
He taught me by example there to see
That it is wrong to marry more than once.
Consider, too, how sharply, for the nonce,
He spoke, rebuking the Samaritan
Beside the well, Christ Jesus, God and man.
"Thou has had five men husband unto thee
And he that even now thou hast," said He,
"Is not thy husband." Such the words that fell;

But what He meant thereby I cannot tell.
Why was her fifth—explain it if you can—
No lawful spouse to the Samaritan?
How many might have had her, then, to wife?
I've never heard an answer all my life
To give the number final definition.
People may guess or frame a supposition,
But I can say for certain, it's no lie,
God bade us all to wax and multiply.
That kindly text I well can understand.
Is not my husband under God's command
To leave his father and mother and take me?
No word of what the number was to be,
Then why not marry two or even eight?
And why speak evil of the married state?

    'Take wise King Solomon of long ago;
We hear he had a thousand wives or so.
And would to God it were allowed to me
To be refreshed, aye, half so much as he!
He must have had a gift of God for wives,
No one to match him in a world of lives!
This noble king, one may as well admit,
On the first night threw many a merry fit
With each of them, he was so much alive.
Blessed be God that I have wedded five!
Welcome the sixth, whenever he appears.
I can't keep continent for years and years.
No sooner than one husband's dead and gone
Some other Christian man shall take me on,

For then, so says the Apostle, I am free
To wed, o' God's name, where it pleases me.
Wedding's no sin, so far as I can learn.
Better it is to marry than to burn.

'What do I care if people choose to see
Scandal in Lamech for his bigamy?
I know that Abraham was a holy man
And Jacob too—I speak as best I can—
Yet each of them, we know, had several brides,
Like many another holy man besides.
Show me a time or text where God disparages
Or sets a prohibition upon marriages
Expressly, let me have it! Show it me!
And where did He command virginity?
I know as well as you do, never doubt it,
All the Apostle Paul has said about it;
He said that as for precepts he had none.
One may advise a woman to be one;
Advice is no commandment in my view.
He left it in our judgement what to do.

'Had God commanded maidenhood to all
Marriage would be condemned beyond recall,
And certainly if seed were never sown,
How ever could virginity be grown?
Paul did not dare pronounce, let matters rest,
His Master having given him no behest.
There's a prize offered for virginity;
Catch as catch can! Who's in for it? Let's see!

'It is not everyone who hears the call;

On whom God wills He lets His power fall.
The Apostle was a virgin, well I know;
Nevertheless, though all his writings show
He wished that everyone were such as he,
It's all mere counsel to virginity.
And as for being married, he lets me do it
Out of indulgence, so there's nothing to it
In marrying me, suppose my husband dead;
There's nothing bigamous in such a bed.
Though it were a good man should never touch
A woman (meaning here in bed and such)
And dangerous to assemble fire and tow
—What this allusion means you all must know—
He only says virginity is fresh,
More perfect than the frailty of the flesh
In married life—except when he and she
Prefer to live in married chastity.

   'I grant it you. I'll never say a word
Decrying maidenhood although preferred
To frequent marriage; there are those who mean
To live in their virginity, as clean
In body as in soul, and never mate.
I'll make no boast about my own estate.
As in a noble household, we are told,
Not every dish and vessel's made of gold,
Some are of wood, yet earn their master's praise,
God calls His folks to Him in many ways.
To each of them God gave His proper gift,
Some this, some that, and left them to make shift.

Virginity is indeed a great perfection,
And married continence, for God's dilection,
But Christ, who of perfection is the well,
Bade not that everyone should go and sell
All that he had and give it to the poor
To follow in His footsteps, that is sure.
He spoke to those that would live perfectly,
And by your leave, my lords, that's not for me.
I will bestow the flower of life, the honey,
Upon the acts and fruit of matrimony.

'Tell me to what conclusion or in aid
Of what were generative organs made?
And for what profit were those creatures wrought?
Trust me, they cannot have been made for naught.
Gloze as you will and plead the explanation
That they were only made for the purgation
Of urine, little things of no avail
Except to know a female from a male,
And nothing else. Did somebody say no?
Experience knows well it isn't so.
The learned may rebuke me, or be loth
To think it so, but they were made for both,
That is to say both use and pleasure in
Engendering, except in case of sin.
Why else the proverb written down and set
In books: "A man must yield his wife her debt"?
What means of paying her can he invent
Unless he use his silly instrument?
It follows they were fashioned at creation

Both to purge urine and for propagation.
   'But I'm not saying everyone is bound
Who has such harness as you heard me expound
To go and use it breeding; that would be
To show too little care for chastity.
Christ was a virgin, fashioned as a man,
And many of his saints since time began
Were ever perfect in their chastity.
I'll have no quarrel with virginity.
Let them be pure wheat loaves of maidenhead
And let us wives be known for barley-bread;
Yet Mark can tell that barley-bread sufficed
To freshen many at the hand of Christ.
In that estate to which God summoned me
I'll persevere; I'm not pernickety.
In wifehood I will use my instrument
As freely as my Maker me it sent.
If I turn difficult, God give me sorrow!
My husband, he shall have it eve and morrow
Whenever he likes to come and pay his debt,
I won't prevent him! I'll have a husband yet
Who shall be both my debtor and my slave
And bear his tribulation to the grave
Upon his flesh, as long as I'm his wife.
For mine shall be the power all his life
Over his proper body, and not he,
Thus the Apostle Paul has told it me,
And bade our husbands they should love us well;

6 There's a command on which I like to dwell . . .'

The Pardoner started up, and thereupon
'Madam,' he said, 'by God and by St. John,
That's noble preaching no one could surpass!
I was about to take a wife; alas!
Am I to buy it on my flesh so dear?
There'll be no marrying for me this year!'
    'You wait,' she said, 'my story's not begun.
You'll taste another brew before I've done;
You'll find it doesn't taste as good as ale;
And when I've finished telling you my tale
Of tribulation in the married life
In which I've been an expert as a wife,
That is to say, myself have been the whip.
So please yourself whether you want to sip
At that same cask of marriage I shall broach.
Be cautious before making the approach,
For I'll give instances, and more than ten.
And those who won't be warned by other men,
By other men shall suffer their correction,
So Ptolemy has said, in this connection.
You read his *Almagest;* you'll find it there.'
    'Madam, I put it to you as a prayer,'
The Pardoner said, 'go on as you began!
Tell us your tale, spare not for any man.
Instruct us younger men in your technique.'
'Gladly,' she said, 'if you will let me speak,
But still I hope the company won't reprove me
Though I should speak as fantasy may move me,
And please don't be offended at my views;

They're really only offered to amuse.

   'Now, gentlemen, I'll go on and tell my tale
And as I hope to drink good wine and ale
I'll tell the truth. Those husbands that I had,
Three of them were good and two were bad.
The three that I call 'good' were rich and old.
They could indeed with difficulty hold
The articles that bound them all to me;
(No doubt you understand my simile).
So help me God, I have to laugh outright
Remembering how I made them work at night!
And faith I set no store by it; no pleasure
It was to me. They'd given me their treasure,
And so I had no need of diligence
Winning their love, or showing reverence.
They loved me well enough, so, heavens above,
Why should I make a dainty of their love?

   'A knowing woman's work is never done
To get a lover if she hasn't one,
But as I had them eating from my hand
And as they'd yielded me their gold and land,
Why then take trouble to provide them pleasure
Unless to profit and amuse my leisure?
I set them so to work, I'm bound to say;
Many a night they sang, "Alack the day!"
Never for them the flitch of bacon though
That some have won in Essex at Dunmow!
I managed them so well by my technique

Each was delighted to go out and seek

And buy some pretty thing for me to wear,
Happy if I as much as spoke them fair.
God knows how spitefully I used to scold them.
   'Listen, I'll tell you how I used to hold them,
You knowing women, who can understand,
First put them in the wrong, and out of hand.
No one can be so bold—I mean no man—
At lies and swearing as a woman can.
This is no news, as you'll have realized,
To knowing ones, but to the misadvised.
A knowing wife if she is worth her salt
Can always prove her husband is at fault,
And even though the fellow may have heard
Some story told him by a little bird
She knows enough to prove the bird is crazy
And get her maid to witness she's a daisy,
With full agreement, scarce solicited.
But listen. Here's the sort of thing I said:
   ' "Now, sir old dotard, what is that you say?
Why is my neighbour's wife so smart and gay?
She is respected everywhere she goes.
I sit at home and have no decent clothes.
Why haunt her house? What are you doing there?
Are you so amorous? Is she so fair?
What, whispering secrets to our maid? For shame,
Sir ancient lecher! Time you dropped that game.
And if I see my gossip or a friend
You scold me like a devil! There's no end
If I as much as stroll towards his house.

Then you come home as drunken as a mouse,
You mount your throne and preach, chapter and verse
—All nonsense—and you tell me it's a curse
To marry a poor woman—she's expensive;
Or if her family's wealthy and extensive
You say it's torture to endure her pride
And melancholy airs, and more beside.
And if she has a pretty face, old traitor,
You says she's game for any fornicator
And ask what likelihood will keep her straight
With all those men who lie about in wait.

  ' "You say that some desire us for our wealth,
Some for our shapeliness, our looks, our health,
Some for our singing, others for our dancing,
Some for our gentleness and dalliant glancing,
And some because our hands are soft and small;
By your account the devil gets us all.

  ' "You say what castle wall can be so strong
As to hold out against a siege for long?
And if her looks are foul you say that she
Is hot for every man that she can see,
Leaping upon them with a spaniel's airs
Until she finds a man to buy her wares.
Never was goose upon the lake so grey
But that she found a gander, so you say.
You say it's hard to keep a girl controlled
If she's the kind that no one wants to hold.
That's what you say as you stump off to bed,
10 You brute! You say no man of sense would wed,

That is, not if he wants to go to Heaven.
Wild thunderbolts and fire from the Seven
Planets descend and break your withered neck!
    ' "You say that buildings falling into wreck,
And smoke, and scolding women, are the three
Things that will drive a man from home. Dear me!
What ails the poor old man to grumble so?
    ' "We women hide our faults but let them show
Once we are safely married, so you say.
There's a fine proverb for a popinjay!
    ' "You say that oxen, asses, hounds and horses
Can be tried out on various ploys and courses;
And basins too, and dishes when you buy them,
Spoons, chairs and furnishings, a man can try them
As he can try a suit of clothes, no doubt,
But no one ever tries a woman out
Until he's married her; old dotard crow!
And then you say she lets her vices show.
    ' "You also say we count it for a crime
Unless you praise our beauty all the time,
Unless you're always poring on our faces
And call us pretty names in public places;
Or if you fail to treat me to a feast
Upon my birthday—presents at the least—
Or to respect my nurse and her grey hairs,
Or be polite to all my maids upstairs
And to my father's cronies and his spies.
That's what you say, old barrelful of lies!
    ' "Then there's our young apprentice, handsome Johnny,

Because he has crisp hair that shines as bonny
As finest gold, and squires me up and down
You show your low suspicions in a frown.
I wouldn't have him, not if you died to-morrow!
  ' "And tell me this, God punish you with sorrow,
Why do you hide the key of coffer doors?
It's just as much my property as yours.
Do you want to make an idiot of your wife?
Now, by the Lord that gave me soul and life,
You shan't have both, you can't be such a noddy
As to think to keep my goods and have my body!
One you must do without, whatever you say.
And do you need to spy on me all day?
I think you'd like to lock me in your coffer!
'Go where you please, dear wife,' you ought to offer,
'Amuse yourself! I shan't give ear to malice,
I know you for a virtuous wife, Dame Alice.'
We cannot love a husband who takes charge
Of where we go. We like to be at large.
  ' "Above all other men may God confer
His blessing on that wise astrologer
Sir Ptolemy who, in his *Almagest*,
Has set this proverb down: 'Of men, the best
And wisest care not who may have in hand
The conduct of the world.' I understand
That means, 'If you've enough, you shouldn't care
How prosperously other people fare.'
Be sure, old dotard, if you call the bluff,
12 You'll get your evening rations right enough.

He's a mean fellow that lets no man handle
His lantern when it's just to light a candle;
He has lost no light, he hasn't felt the strain;
And you have light enough, so why complain?
 ' "And when a woman tries a mild display
In dress or costly ornament, you say
It is a danger to her chastity,
And then, bad luck to you, start making free
With Bible tags in the Apostle's name;
'And in like manner, chastely and with shame,
You women should adorn yourselves,' said he,
'And not with braided hair or jewelry,
With pearl or golden ornament.' What next!
I'll pay as much attention to your text
And rubric in such things as would a gnat.
 ' "And once you said that I was like a cat,
For if you singe a cat it will not roam
And that's the way to keep a cat at home.
But when she feels her fur is sleek and gay
She can't be kept indoors for half a day
But off she takes herself as dusk is falling
To show her fur and go a-caterwauling.
Which means if I feel gay, as you suppose,
I shall run out to show my poor old clothes.
 ' "Silly old fool! You and your private spies!
Go on, beg Argus with his hundred eyes
To be my bodyguard, that's better still!
But yet he shan't, I say, against my will.
I'll pull him by the beard, and believe you me!

' "And once you said that principally three
Misfortunes trouble earth, east, west and north,
And no man living could endure a fourth.
My dear sir shrew, Jesu cut short your life!
You preach away and say a hateful wife
Is reckoned to be one of these misfortunes.
Is there no other trouble that importunes
The world and that your parables could condemn?
Must an unhappy wife be one of them?

' "Then you compared a woman's love to Hell,
To barren land where water will not dwell,
And you compared it to a quenchless fire,
The more it burns the more is its desire
To burn up everything that burnt can be.
You say that just as worms destroy a tree
A wife destroys her husband and contrives,
As husbands know, the ruin of their lives."

'Such was the way, my lords, you understand
I kept my older husbands well in hand.
I told them they were drunk and their unfitness
To judge my conduct forced me to take witness
That they were lying. Johnny and my niece
Would back me up. O Lord, I wrecked their peace,
Innocent as they were, without remorse!
For I could bite and whinney like a horse
And launch complaints when things were all my fault;
I'd have been lost if I had called a halt.
First to the mill is first to grind your corn;
I attacked first and they were overborne,

Glad to apologize and even suing
Pardon for what they'd never thought of doing.

   'I'd tackle one for wenching, out of hand,
Although so ill the man could hardly stand,
Yet he felt flattered in his heart because
He thought it showed how fond of him I was.
I swore that all my walking out at night
Was just to keep his wenching well in sight.
That was a dodge that made me shake with mirth;
But all such wit is given us at birth.
Lies, tears and spinning are the things God gives
By nature to a woman, while she lives.
So there's one thing at least that I can boast,
That in the end I always ruled the roast;
Cunning or force was sure to make them stumble,
And always keeping up to a steady grumble.

   'But bed-time above all was their misfortune;
That was the place to scold them and importune
And baulk their fun. I never would abide
In bed with them if hands began to slide
Till they had promised ransom, paid a fee:
And then I let them do their nicety.
And so I tell this tale to every man,
"It's all for sale and let him win who can."
No empty-handed man can lure a bird.
His pleasures were my profit; I concurred,
Even assumed fictitious appetite,
Though bacon never gave me much delight.
And that's the very fact that made me chide them.

And had the Pope been sitting there beside them
I wouldn't have spared them at their very table,
But paid them out as far as I was able.
I say, so help me God Omnipotent,
Were I to make my will and testament
I owe them nothing, paid them word for word
Putting my wits to use, and they preferred
To give it up and take it for the best
For otherwise they would have got no rest.
Though they might glower like a maddened beast
They got no satisfaction, not the least.

   'I then would say, "My dear, just take a peep!
What a meek look on Willikin our sheep!
Come nearer, husband, let me kiss your cheek;
You should be just as patient, just as meek;
Sweeten your heart. Your conscience needs a probe.
You're fond of preaching patience out of Job,
And so be patient; practise what you preach,
And if you don't, my dear, we'll have to teach
You that it's nice to have a quiet life.
One of us must be master, man or wife,
And since a man's more reasonable, he
Should be the patient one, you must agree.

   ' "What ails you, man, to grumble so and groan?
Just that you want my what-not all your own?
Why, take it all, man, take it, every bit!
St Peter, what a love you have for it!
For if I were to sell my *belle chose*,

16 I could go walking fresher than a rose;

But I will keep it for your private tooth.
By God, you are to blame, and that's the truth."
   'That's how my first three husbands were undone.
Now let me tell you of my last but one.

   'He was a reveller, was number four;
That is to say he kept a paramour.
Young, strong and stubborn, I was full of rage
And jolly as a magpie in a cage.
Play me the harp and I would dance and sing,
Believe me, like a nightingale in spring,
If I had had a draught of sweetened wine.
   'Metellius, that filthy lout—the swine
Who snatched a staff and took his woman's life
For drinking wine—if I had been his wife
He never would have daunted me from drink.
Whenever I take wine I have to think
Of Venus, for as cold engenders hail
A lecherous mouth begets a lecherous tail.
A woman in her cups has no defence,
As lechers know from long experience.
   'But Christ! Whenever it comes back to me,
When I recall my youth and jollity,
It fairly warms the cockles of my heart!
This very day I feel a pleasure start,
Yes, I can feel it tickling at the root.
Lord, how it does me good! I've had my fruit,
I've had my world and time, I've had my fling!
But age that comes to poison everything
Has taken all my beauty and my pith.

Well, let it go, the devil go therewith!
The flour is gone, there is no more to say,
And I must sell the bran as best I may;
But still I mean to find my way to fun. . . .
No let me tell you of my last but one.

'I told you how it filled my heart with spite
To see another woman his delight,
By God and all His saints I made it good!
I carved him out a cross of the same wood,
Not with my body in a filthy way,
But certainly by seeming rather gay
To others, frying him in his own grease
Of jealousy and rage; he got no peace.
By God on earth I was his purgatory,
For which I hope his soul may be in glory.
God knows he sang a sorry tune, he flinched,
And bitterly enough, when the shoe pinched.
And God and he alone can say how grim,
How many were the ways I tortured him.

'He died when I came back from Jordan Stream
And he lies buried under the rood-beam,
Albeit that his tomb can scarce supply us
With such a show as that of King Darius
—Apelles sculped it in a sumptuous taste—
Expensive funerals are just a waste.
Farewell to him, God give his spirit rest!
He's in his grave, he's nailed up in his chest.

'Now of my fifth, last husband let me tell.
God never let his soul be sent to Hell!

And yet he was my worst, and many a blow
He struck me still can ache along my row
Of ribs, and will until my dying day.
    'But in our bed he was so fresh and gay,
So coaxing, so persuasive. . . . Heaven knows
Whenever he wanted it—my *belle chose*—
Though he had beaten me in every bone
He still could wheedle me to love, I own.
I think I loved him best, I'll tell no lie.
He was disdainful in his love, that's why.
We women have a curious fantasy
In such affairs, or so it seems to me.
When something's difficult, or can't be had,
We crave and cry for it all day like mad.
Forbid a thing, we pine for it all night,
Press fast upon us and we take to flight;
We use disdain in offering our wares.
A throng of buyers sends prices up at fairs,
Cheap goods have little value, they suppose;
And that's a thing that every woman knows.
    'My fifth and last—God keep his soul in health!
The one I took for love and not for wealth,
Had been at Oxford not so long before
But had left school and gone to lodge next door,
Yes, it was to my godmother's he'd gone.
God bless her soul! *Her* name was Alison.
She knew my heart and more of what I thought
Than did the parish priest, and so she ought!
She was my confidante, I told her all.

For had my husband pissed against a wall
Or done some crime that would have cost his life,
To her and to another worthy wife
And to my niece, because I loved her well,
I'd have told everything there was to tell.
And so I often did, and Heaven knows
It used to set him blushing like a rose
For shame, and he would blame his lack of sense
In telling me secrets of such consequence.

'And so one time it happened that in Lent,
As I so often did, I rose and went
To see her, ever wanting to be gay
And go a-strolling, March, April and May,
From house to house for chat and village malice.

'Johnny (the boy from Oxford) and Dame Alice
And I myself, into the fields we went.
My husband was in London all that Lent;
All the more fun for me—I only mean
The fun of seeing people and being seen
By cocky lads; for how was I to know
Where or what graces Fortune might bestow?
And so I made a round of visitations,
Went to processions, festivals, orations,
Preachments and pilgrimages, watched the carriages
They use for plays and pageants, went to marriages,
And always wore my gayest scarlet dress.

'These worms, these moths, these mites, I must confess,
Got little chance to eat it, by the way.
20 Why not? Because I wore it every day.

'Now let me tell you all that came to pass.
We sauntered in the meadows through the grass
Toying and dallying to such extent,
Johnny and I, that I grew provident
And I suggested, were I ever free
And made a widow, he should marry me.
And certainly—I do not mean to boast—
I ever was more provident than most
In marriage matters and in other such.
I never think a mouse is up to much
That only has one hole in all the house;
If that should fail, well, it's good-bye the mouse.

'I let him think I was as one enchanted
(That was a trick my godmother implanted)
And told him I had dreamt the night away
Thinking of him, and dreamt that as I lay
He tried to kill me. Blood had drenched the bed.

' "But still it was a lucky dream," I said,
"For blood betokens gold as I recall."
It was a lie. I hadn't dreamt at all.
'Twas from my godmother I learnt my lore
In matters such as that, and many more.

'Well, let me see . . . what had I to explain?
Aha! By God, I've got the thread again.

'When my fourth husband lay upon his bier
I wept all day and looked as drear as drear,
As widows must, for it is quite in place,
And with a handkerchief I hid my face.
Now that I felt provided with a mate

I wept but little, I need hardly state.
  'To church they bore my husband on the morrow
With all the neighbours round him venting sorrow,
And one of them of course was handsome Johnny.
So help me God, I thought he looked so bonny
Behind the coffin! Heavens, what a pair
Of legs he had! Such feet, so clean and fair!
I gave my whole heart up, for him to hold.
He was, I think, some twenty winters old,
And I was forty then, to tell the truth.
But still, I always had a coltish tooth.
Yes, I'm gap-toothed; it suits me well I feel,
It is the print of Venus and her seal.
So help me God I was a lusty one,
Fair, young and well-to-do, and full of fun!
And truly, as my husbands said to me
I had the finest *quoniam* that might be.
For Venus sent me feeling from the stars
And my heart's boldness came to me from Mars.
Venus gave me desire and lecherousness
And Mars my hardihood, or so I guess,
Born under Taurus and with Mars therein.
Alas, alas, that ever love was sin!
I ever followed natural inclination
Under the power of my constellation
And was unable to deny, in truth,
My chamber of Venus to a likely youth.
The mark of Mars is still upon my face
And also in another privy place.

For as I may be saved by God above,
I never used discretion when in love
But ever followed on my appetite,
Whether the lad was short, long, black or white.
Little I cared, if he was fond of me,
How poor he was, or what his rank might be.

   'What shall I say? Before the month was gone
This gay young student, my delightful John,
Had married me in solemn festival.
I handed him the money, lands and all
That ever had been given me before;
This I repented later, more and more.
None of my pleasures would he let me seek.
By God, he smote me once upon the cheek
Because I tore a page out of his book,
And that's the reason why I'm deaf. But look,
Stubborn I was, just like a lioness;
As to my tongue, a very wrangleress.
I went off gadding as I had before
From house to house, however much he swore.
Because of that he used to preach and scold,
Drag Roman history up from days of old,
How one Simplicius Gallus left his wife,
Deserting her completely all his life,
Only for poking out her head one day
Without a hat, upon the public way.

   'Some other Roman—I forget his name—
Because his wife went to a summer's game
Without his knowledge, left her in the lurch.

'And he would take the Bible up and search
For proverbs in Ecclesiasticus,
Particularly one that has it thus:
"Suffer no wicked woman to gad about."
And then would come the saying (need you doubt?)
  A man who seeks to build his house of sallows,
  A man who spurs a blind horse over fallows,
  Or lets his wife make pilgrimage to Hallows,
  Is worthy to be hanged upon the gallows.
But all for naught. I didn't give a hen
For all his proverbs and his wise old men.
Nor would I take rebuke at any price;
I hate a man who points me out my vice,
And so, God knows, do many more than I.
That drove him raging mad, you may rely.
Nor more would I forbear him, I can promise.

  'Now let me tell you truly by St Thomas
About that book and why I tore the page
And how he smote me deaf in very rage.

  'He had a book, he kept it on a shelf,
And night and day he read it to himself
And laughed aloud, although it was quite serious.
He called it *Theophrastus and Valerius.*
There was another Roman, much the same,
A cardinal; St Jerome was his name.
He wrote a book against Jovinian,
Bound up together with Tertullian,
Chrysippus, Trotula and Heloise,

An abbess, lived near Paris. And with these

Were bound the parables of Solomon,
With Ovid's *Art of Love* another one.
All these were bound together in one book
And day and night he used to take a look
At what it said, when he had time and leisure
Or had no occupation but his pleasure,
Which was to read this book of wicked wives;
He knew more legends of them and their lives
Than there are good ones mentioned in the Bible.
For take my word for it, there is no libel
On women that the clergy will not paint,
Except when writing of a woman-saint,
But never good of other women, though.
Who called the lion savage? Do you know?
By God, if women had but written stories
Like those the clergy keep in oratories,
More had been written of man's wickedness
Than all the sons of Adam could redress.
Children of Mercury and we of Venus
Keep up the contrariety between us;
Mercury stands for wisdom, thrift and science,
Venus for revel, squandering and defiance.
Their several natures govern their direction;
One rises when the other's in dejection.
So Mercury is desolate when halted
In *Pisces*, just where Venus is exalted,
And Venus falls where Mercury is raised,
And women therefore never can be praised
By learned men, old scribes who cannot do

The works of Venus more than my old shoe.
These in their dotage sit them down to frowse
And say that women break their marriage-vows!

   'Now to my purpose as I told you; look,
Here's how I got a beating for a book.
One evening Johnny, glowering with ire,
Sat with his book and read it by the fire.
And first he read of Eve whose wickedness
Brought all mankind to sorrow and distress,
Root-cause why Jesus Christ Himself was slain
And gave His blood to buy us back again.
Aye, there's the text where you expressly find
That woman brought the loss of all mankind.

   'He read me then how Samson as he slept
Was shorn of all his hair by her he kept,
And by that treachery Samson lost his eyes.
And then he read me, if I tell no lies,
All about Hercules and Deianire;
She tricked him into setting himself on fire.

   'He left out nothing of the miseries
Occasioned by his wives to Socrates.
Xantippe poured a piss-pot on his head.
The silly man sat still, as he were dead,
Wiping his head, but dared no more complain
Than say, "Ere thunder stops, down comes the rain."

   'Next of Pasiphaë the Queen of Crete;
For wickedness he thought that story sweet;
Fie, say no more! It has a grisly sting,
Her horrible lust. How could she do the thing!

'And then he told of Clytemnestra's lechery
And how she made her husband die by treachery.
He read that story with a great devotion.

'He read me what occasioned the commotion
By which Amphiaraüs lost his life;
My husband had a legend about his wife
Eriphyle, who for a gaud in gold
Went to the Greeks in secret, and she told
Them where to find him, in what hiding-place.
At Thebes it was; he met with sorry grace.

'Of Livia and Lucilia then he read,
And both of course had killed their husbands dead,
The one for love, the other out of hate.
Livia prepared some poison for him late
One evening and she killed him out of spite,
Lucilia out of lecherous delight.
For she, in order he might only think
Of her, prepared an aphrodisiac drink;
He drank it and was dead before the morning.
Such is the fate of husbands; it's a warning.

'And then he told how one Latumius
Lamented to his comrade Arrius
That in his orchard-plot there grew a tree
On which his wives had hanged themselves, all three,
Or so he said, out of some spite or other;
To which this Arrius replied, "Dear brother,
Give me a cutting from that blessed tree
And planted in my garden it shall be!"

'Of wives of later date he also read,

How some had killed their husbands when in bed,
Then night-long with their lechers played the whore,
While the poor corpse lay fresh upon the floor.
 'One drove a nail into her husband's brain
While he was sleeping, and the man was slain;
Others put poison in their husband's drink.
He spoke more harm of us than heart can think
And knew more proverbs too, for what they're worth,
Than there are blades of grass upon the earth.
 ' "Better," says he, "to share your habitation
With lion, dragon, or abomination
Than with a woman given to reproof.
Better," says he, "take refuge on the roof
Than with an angry wife, down in the house;
They are so wicked and cantankerous
They hate the things their husbands like," he'd say.
"A woman always casts her shame away
When she casts off her smock, and that's in haste.
A pretty woman, if she isn't chaste,
Is like a golden ring in a sow's snout."
 'Who could imagine, who could figure out
The torture in my heart? It reached the top
And when I saw that he would never stop
Reading this cursed book, all night no doubt,
I suddenly grabbed and tore three pages out
Where he was reading, at the very place,
And fisted such a buffet in his face
That backwards down into our fire he fell.
 'Then like a maddened lion, with a yell

He started up and smote me on the head,
And down I fell upon the floor for dead.
  'And when he saw how motionless I lay
He was aghast and would have fled away,
But in the end I started to come to.
"O have you murdered me, you robber, you,
To get my land?" I said. "Was that the game?
Before I'm dead I'll kiss you all the same."

  'He came up close and kneeling gently down
He said, "My love, my dearest Alison,
So help me God, I never again will hit
You, love; and if I did, you asked for it.
Forgive me!" But for all he was so meek,
I up at once and smote him on the cheek
And said, "Take that to level up the score!
Now let me die, I can't speak any more."

  'We had a mort of trouble and heavy weather
But in the end we made it up together.
He gave the bridle over to my hand,
Gave me the government of house and land,
Of tongue and fist, indeed of all he'd got.
I made him burn that book upon the spot.
And when I'd mastered him, and out of deadlock
Secured myself the sovereignty in wedlock,
And when he said, "My own and truest wife,
Do as you please for all the rest of life,
But guard your honour and my good estate,"
From that day forward there was no debate.
So help me God I was as kind to him

As any wife from Denmark to the rim
Of India, and as true. And he to me.
And I pray God that sits in majesty
To bless his soul and fill it with his glory.
Now, if you listen, I will tell my story.'

Words Between the Summoner and the Friar

The Friar laughed when he had heard all this.
'Well, Ma'am,' he said, 'as God may send me bliss,
This is a long preamble to a tale!'
But when the Summoner heard the Friar rail,
'Just look!' he cried, 'by the two arms of God!
These meddling friars are always on the prod!
Don't we all know a friar and a fly
Go prod and buzz in every dish and pie!
What do you mean with your "preambulation"?
Amble yourself, trot, do a meditation!
You're spoiling all our fun with your commotion.'
The Friar smiled and said, 'Is that your motion?
I promise on my word before I go
To find occasion for a tale or so
About a summoner that will make us laugh.'
'Well, damn your eyes, and on my own behalf,'
The Summoner answered, 'mine be damned as well
If I can't think of several tales to tell
About the friars that will make you mourn
Before we get as far as Sittingbourne.
30

Have you no patience? Look, he's in a huff!'
   Our Host called out, 'Be quiet, that's enough!
Shut up, and let the woman tell her tale.
You must be drunk, you've taken too much ale.
Now, Ma'am, you go ahead and no demur.'
'All right,' she said, 'it's just as you prefer,
If I have licence from this worthy friar.'
'Nothing,' said he, 'that I should more desire.'

The Wife of Bath's Tale

When good King Arthur ruled in ancient days
(A king that every Briton loves to praise)
This was a land brim-full of fairy folk.
The Elf-Queen and her courtiers joined and broke
Their elfin dance on many a green mead,
Or so was the opinion once, I read,
Hundreds of years ago, in days of yore.
But no one now sees fairies any more.
For now the saintly charity and prayer
Of holy friars seem to have purged the air;
They search the countryside through field and stream
As thick as motes that speckle a sun-beam,
Blessing the halls, the chambers, kitchens, bowers,
Cities and boroughs, castles, courts and towers,
Thorpes, barns and stables, outhouses and dairies,
And that's the reason why there are no fairies.
Wherever there was wont to walk an elf

To-day there walks the holy friar himself
As evening falls or when the daylight springs,
Saying his mattins and his holy things,
Walking his limit round from town to town.
Women can now go safely up and down
By every bush or under every tree;
There is no other incubus but he,
So there is really no one else to hurt you
And he will do no more than take your virtue.

    Now it so happened, I began to say,
Long, long ago in good King Arthur's day,
There was a knight who was a lusty liver.
One day as he came riding from the river
He saw a maiden walking all forlorn
Ahead of him, alone as she was born.
And of that maiden, spite of all she said,
By very force he took her maidenhead.

    This act of violence made such a stir,
So much petitioning to the king for her,
That he condemned the knight to lose his head
By course of law. He was as good as dead
(It seems that then the statutes took that view)
But that the queen, and other ladies too,
Implored the king to exercise his grace
So ceaselessly, he gave the queen the case
And granted her his life, and she could choose
Whether to show him mercy or refuse.

    The queen returned him thanks with all her might,
And then she sent a summons to the knight

At her convenience, and expressed her will:
'You stand, for such is the position still,
In no way certain of your life,' said she,
'Yet you shall live if you can answer me:
What is the thing that women most desire?
Beware the axe and say as I require.

'If you can't answer on the moment, though,
I will concede you this: you are to go
A twelvemonth and a day to seek and learn
Sufficient answer, then you shall return.
I shall take gages from you to extort
Surrender of your body to the court.'

Sad was the knight and sorrowfully sighed,
But there! All other choices were denied,
And in the end he chose to go away
And to return after a year and day
Armed with such answer as there might be sent
To him by God. He took his leave and went.

He knocked at every house, searched every place,
Yes, anywhere that offered hope of grace.
What could it be that women wanted most?
But all the same he never touched a coast,
Country or town in which there seemed to be
Any two people willing to agree.

Some said that women wanted wealth and treasure,
'Honour,' said some, some 'Jollity and pleasure,'
Some 'Gorgeous clothes' and other 'Fun in bed,'
'To be oft widowed and remarried,' said
Others again, and some that what most mattered

Was that we should be cossetted and flattered.
That's very near the truth, it seems to me;
A man can win us best with flattery.
To dance attendance on us, make a fuss,
Ensnares us all, the best and worst of us.

Some say the things we most desire are these:
Freedom to do exactly as we please,
With no one to reprove our faults and lies,
Rather to have one call us good and wise.
Truly there's not a woman in ten score
Who has a fault, and someone rubs the sore,
But she will kick if what he says is true;
You try it out and you will find so too.
However vicious we may be within
We like to be thought wise and void of sin.
Others assert we women find it sweet
When we are thought depandable, discreet
And secret, firm of purpose and controlled,
Never betraying things that we are told.
But that's not worth the handle of a rake;
Women conceal a thing? For Heaven's sake!
Remember Midas? Will you hear the tale?

Among some other little things, now stale,
Ovid relates that under his long hair
The unhappy Midas grew a splendid pair
Of ass's ears; as subtly as he might,
He kept his foul deformity from sight;
Save for his wife, there was not one that knew.
He loved her best, and trusted in her too.

He begged her not to tell a living creature
That he possessed so horrible a feature.
And she—she swore, were all the world to win,
She would not do such villainy and sin
As saddle her husband with so foul a name;
Besides to speak would be to share the shame.
Nevertheless she thought she would have died
Keeping this secret bottled up inside;
It seemed to swell her heart and she, no doubt,
Thought it was on the point of bursting out.

    Fearing to speak of it to woman or man,
Down to a reedy marsh she quickly ran
And reached the sedge. Her heart was all on fire
And, as a bittern bumbles in the mire,
She whispered to the water, near the ground,
'Betray me not, O water, with thy sound!
To thee alone I tell it: it appears
My husband has a pair of ass's ears!
Ah! My heart's well again, the secret's out!
I could no longer keep it, not a doubt.'
And so you see, although we may hold fast
A little while, it must come out at last,
We can't keep secrets; as for Midas, well,
Read Ovid for his story; he will tell.

    This knight that I am telling you about
Perceived at last he never would find out
What it could be that women loved the best.
Faint was the soul within his sorrowful breast,
As home he went, he dared no longer stay;

His year was up and now it was the day.
   As he rode home in a dejected mood
Suddenly, at the margin of a wood,
He saw a dance upon the leafy floor
Of four and twenty ladies, nay, and more.
Eagerly he approached, in hope to learn
Some words of wisdom ere he should return;
But lo! Before he came to where they were,
Dancers and dance all vanished into air!
There wasn't a living creature to be seen
Save one old woman crouched upon the green.
A fouler-looking creature I suppose
Could scarcely be imagined. She arose
And said, 'Sir knight, there's no way on from here.
Tell me what you are looking for, my dear,
For peradventure that were best for you;
We old, old women know a thing or two.'
   'Dear Mother,' said the knight, 'alack the day!
I am as good as dead if I can't say
What thing it is that women most desire;
If you could tell me I would pay your hire.'
'Give me your hand,' she said, 'and swear to do
Whatever I shall next require of you
—If so to do should lie within your might—
And you shall know the answer before night.'
'Upon my honour,' he answered, 'I agree.'
'Then,' said the crone, 'I dare to guarantee
Your life is safe; I shall make good my claim.
36 Upon my life the queen will say the same.

Show me the very proudest of them all
In costly coverchief or jewelled caul
That dare say no to what I have to teach.
Let us go forward without further speech.'
And then she crooned her gospel in his ear
And told him to be glad and not to fear.

They came to court. This knight, in full array,
Stood forth and said, 'O Queen, I've kept my day
And kept my word and have my answer ready.'

There sat the noble matrons and the heady
Young girls, and widows too, that have the grace
Of wisdom, all assembled in that place,
And there the queen herself was throned to hear
And judge his answer. Then the knight drew near
And silence was commanded through the hall.

The queen gave order he should tell them all
What thing it was that women wanted most.
He stood not silent like a beast or post,
But gave his answer with the ringing word
Of a man's voice and the assembly heard:

'My liege and lady, in general,' said he,
'A woman wants the self-same sovereignty
Over her husband as over her lover,
And master him; he must not be above her.
That is your greatest wish, whether you kill
Or spare me; please yourself. I wait your will.'

In all the court not one that shook her head
Or contradicted what the knight had said;
Maid, wife and widow cried, 'He's saved his life!'

And on the word up started the old wife,
The one the knight saw sitting on the green,
And cried, 'Your mercy, sovereign lady queen!
Before the court disperses, do me right!
'Twas I who taught this answer to the knight,
For which he swore, and pledged his honour to it,
That the first thing I asked of him he'd do it,
So far as it should lie within his might.
Before this court I ask you then, sir knight,
To keep your word and take me for your wife;
For well you know that I have saved your life.
If this be false, deny it on your sword!'

'Alas!' he said, 'Old lady, by the Lord
I know indeed that such was my behest,
But for God's love think of a new request,
Take all my goods, but leave my body free.'
'A curse on us,' she said, 'if I agree!
I may be foul, I may be poor and old,
Yet will not choose to be, for all the gold
That's bedded in the earth or lies above,
Less than your wife, nay, than your very love!'

'My love?' said he. 'By heaven, my damnation!
Alas that any of my race and station
Should ever make so foul a misalliance!'
Yet in the end his pleading and defiance
All went for nothing, he was forced to wed.
He takes his ancient wife and goes to bed.

Now peradventure some may well suspect
A lack of care in me since I neglect

To tell of the rejoicings and display
Made at the feast upon their wedding-day.
I have but a short answer to let fall;
I say there was no joy or feast at all,
Nothing but heaviness of heart and sorrow.
He married her in private on the morrow
And all day long stayed hidden like an owl,
It was such torture that his wife looked foul.

   Great was the anguish churning in his head
When he and she were piloted to bed;
He wallowed back and forth in desperate style.
His ancient wife lay smiling all the while;
At last she said, 'Bless us! Is this, my dear,
How knights and wives get on together here?
Are these the laws of good King Arthur's house?
Are knights of his all so contemptuous?
I am your own beloved and your wife,
And I am she, indeed, that saved your life;
And certainly I never did you wrong.
Then why, this first of nights, so sad a song?
You're carrying on as if you were half-witted
Say, for God's love, what sin have I committed?
I'll put things right if you tell me how.'

   'Put right?' he cried. 'That never can be now!
Nothing can ever be put right again!
You're old, and so abominably plain,
So poor to start with, so low-bred to follow;
It's little wonder if I twist and wallow!
God, that my heart would burst within my breast!'

'Is that," said she, 'the cause of your unrest?'
'Yes, certainly,' he said, 'and can you wonder?'
'I could set right what you suppose a blunder,
That's if I cared to, in a day or two,
If I were shown more courtesy by you.
Just now,' she said, 'you spoke of gentle birth,
Such as descends from ancient wealth and worth.
If that's the claim you make for gentlemen
Such arrogance is hardly worth a hen.
Whoever loves to work for virtuous ends,
Public and private, and who most intends
To do what deeds of gentleness he can,
Take him to be the greatest gentleman.
Christ wills we take our gentleness from Him,
Not from a wealth of ancestry long dim,
Though they bequeath their whole establishment
By which we claim to be of high descent.
Our Fathers cannot make us a bequest
Of all those virtues that became them best
And earned for them the name of gentlemen,
But bade us follow them as best we can.

'Thus the wise poet of the Florentines,
Dante by name, has written in these lines,
For such is the opinion Dante launches:
"Seldom arises by these slender branches
Prowess of men, for it is God, no less,
Wills us to claim of Him our gentleness."
For of our parents nothing can we claim
40 Save temporal things, and these may hurt and maim.

'But everyone knows this as well as I;
For if gentility were implanted by
The natural course of lineage down the line,
Public or private, could it cease to shine
In doing the fair work of gentle deed?
No vice or villainy could then bear seed.

'Take the fire and carry it to the darkest house
Between this kingdom and the Caucasus,
And shut the doors on it and leave it there,
It will burn on, and it will burn as fair
As if ten thousand men were there to see,
For fire will keep its nature and degree,
I can assure you, sir, until it dies.

'But gentleness, as you will recognize,
Is not annexed in nature to possessions.
Men fail in living up to their professions;
But fire never ceases to be fire.
God knows you'll often find, if you enquire,
Some lording full of villainy and shame.
If you would be esteemed for the mere name
Of having been by birth a gentleman
And stemming from some virtuous, noble clan,
And do not live yourself by gentle deed
Or take your father's noble code and creed,
You are no gentleman, though duke or earl.
Vice and bad manners are what make a churl.

'Gentility is only the renown
For bounty that your fathers handed down,
Quite foreign to your person, not your own;

Gentility must come from God alone.
That we are gentle comes to us by grace
And by no means is it bequeathed with place.
   'Reflect how noble (says Valerius)
Was Tullius surnamed Hostilius,
Who rose from poverty to nobleness.
And read Boethius, Seneca no less,
Thus they express themselves and are agreed:
"Gentle is he that does a gentle deed."
And therefore, my dear husband, I conclude
That even if my ancestors were rude,
Yet God on high—and so I hope He will—
Can grant me grace to live in virtue still,
A gentlewoman only when beginning
To live in virtue and to shrink from sinning.
   'As for my poverty which you reprove,
Almighty God Himself in whom we move,
Believe and have our being, chose a life
Of poverty, and every man or wife
Nay, every child can see our Heavenly King
Would never stoop to choose a shameful thing.
No shame in poverty if the heart is gay,
As Seneca and all the learned say.
He who accepts his poverty unhurt
I'd say is rich although he lacked a shirt.
But truly poor are they who whine and fret
And covet what they cannot hope to get.
And he that, having nothing, covets not,
Is rich, though you may think he is a sot.

'True poverty can find a song to sing.
Juvenal says a pleasant little thing:
"The poor can dance and sing in the relief
Of having nothing that will tempt a thief."
Though it be hateful, poverty is good,
A great incentive to a livelihood,
And a great help to our capacity
For wisdom, if accepted patiently.
Poverty is, though wanting in estate,
A kind of wealth that none calumniate.
Poverty often, when the heart is lowly,
Brings one to God and teaches what is holy,
Gives knowledge of oneself and even lends
A glass by which to see one's truest friends.
And since it's no offence, let me be plain;
Do not rebuke my poverty again.

'Lastly you taxed me, sir, with being old.
Yet even if you never had been told
By ancient books, you gentlemen engage
Yourselves in honour to respect old age.
To call an old man "father" shows good breeding,
And this could be supported from my reading.

'You say I'm old and fouler than a fen.
You need not fear to be a cuckold, then.
Filth and old age, I'm sure you will agree,
Are powerful wardens over chastity.
Nevertheless, well knowing your delights,
I shall fulfil your worldly appetites.

'You have two choices; which one will you try?

43

To have me old and ugly till I die,
But still a loyal, true, and humble wife
That never will displease you all her life,
Or would you rather I were young and pretty
And chance your arm what happens in a city
Where friends will visit you because of me,
Yes, and in other places too, maybe.
Which would you have? The choice is all your own.'

The knight thought long, and with a piteous groan
At last he said, with all the care in life,
'My lady and my love, my dearest wife,
I leave the matter to your wise decision.
You make the choice yourself, for the provision
Of what may be agreeable and rich
In honour to us both, I don't care which;
Whatever pleases you suffices me.'

'And have I won the mastery?' said she,
'Since I'm to choose and rule as I think fit?'
'Certainly, wife,' he answered her, 'that's it.'
'Kiss me," she cried. 'No quarrels! On my oath
And word of honour, you shall find me both,
That is, both fair and faithful as a wife;
May I go howling mad and take my life
Unless I prove to be as good and true
As ever wife was since the world was new!
And if to-morrow when the sun's above
I seem less fair than any lady-love,
Than any queen or empress east or west,
44 Do with my life and death as you think best.

Cast up the curtain, husband. Look at me!'
   And when indeed the knight had looked to see,
Lo, she was young and lovely, rich in charms.
In ecstasy he caught her in his arms,
His heart went bathing in a bath of blisses
And melted in a hundred thousand kisses,
And she responded in the fullest measure
With all that could delight or give him pleasure.
   So they lived ever after to the end
In perfect bliss; and may Christ Jesus send
Us husbands meek and young and fresh in bed,
And grace to overbid them when we wed.
And—Jesu hear my prayer!—cut short the lives
Of those who won't be governed by their wives;
And all old, angry niggards of their pence,
God send them soon a very pestilence!

THE MILLER'S TALE

Words Between the Host and the Miller

When we had heard the tale the Knight had told,
Not one among the pilgrims, young or old,
But said it was indeed a noble story
Worthy to be remembered for its glory,
And it especially pleased the gentlefolk.

Our Host began to laugh and swore in joke:
'It's going well, we've opened up the bale;
Now, let me see. Who'll tell another tale?
Upon my soul the game has begun well!
Come on, Sir Monk, if you've a tale to tell,
Repay the Knight a little for his tale!'

The Miller, very drunk and rather pale,
Was straddled on his horse half-on half-off
And in no mood for manners or to doff
His hood or hat, or wait on any man,
But in a voice like Pilate's he began
To huff and swear. 'By blood and bones and belly,
I've got a noble story I can tell 'ee,
I'll pay the Knight his wages, not the Monk.'

Our Host perceived at once that he was drunk
And said, 'Now hold on, Robin, dear old brother;
We'll get some better man to tell another;
You wait a bit. Let's have some common sense.'
'God's soul, I won't!' said he. 'At all events
I mean to talk, or else I'll go my way.'
Our Host replied, 'Well, blast you then, you may.
You fool! Your wits have gone beyond recall.'

'Now listen,' said the Miller, 'one and all,
To what I have to say. But first I'm bound
To say I'm drunk, I know it by my sound.
And if the words get muddled in my tale
Just put it down to too much Southwark ale.
I will relate a legend and a life
46 Of an old carpenter and of his wife,

And how a student came and set his cap . . .'
    The Reeve looked up and shouted, 'Shut your trap!
Give over with your drunken harlotry.
It is a sin and foolishness,' said he,
'To slander any man or bring a scandal
On wives in general. Why can't you handle
Some other tale? There's other things beside.'
    To this the drunken Miller then replied,
'My dear old brother Oswald, such is life.
A man's no cuckold if he has no wife.
For all that, I'm not saying you are one;
There's many virtuous wives, all said and done,
Ever a thousand good for one that's bad,
As well you know yourself, unless you're mad.
Why are you angry? What is this to-do?
I have a wife, God knows, as well as you,
Yet not for all the oxen in my plough
Would I engage to take it on me now
To think myself a cuckold, just because . . .
I'm pretty sure I'm not and never was.
One shouldn't be too inquisitive in life
Either about God's secrets or one's wife.
You'll find God's plenty all you could desire;
Of the remainder, better not enquire.'
    What can I add? The Miller had begun,
He would not hold his peace for anyone,
But told his churl's tale his own way, I fear.
And I regret I must repeat it here,
And so I beg of all who are refined

For God's love not to think me ill-inclined
Or evil in my purpose. I rehearse
Their tales as told, for better or for worse,
For else I should be false to what occurred.
So if this tale had better not be heard,
Just turn the page and choose another sort;
You'll find them here in plenty, long and short;
Many historical, that will profess
Morality, good breeding, saintliness.
Do not blame me if you should choose amiss.
The Miller was a churl, I've told you this,
So was the Reeve, and other some as well,
And harlotry was all they had to tell.
Consider then and hold me free of blame;
And why be serious about a game?

The Miller's Tale

Some time ago there was a rich old codger
Who lived in Oxford and who took a lodger.
The fellow was a carpenter by trade,
His lodger a poor student who had made
Some studies in the arts, but all his fancy
Turned to astrology and geomancy,
And he could deal with certain propositions
And make a forecast under some conditions
About the likelihood of drought or showers
For those who asked at favourable hours,

Or put a question how their luck would fall
In this or that, I can't describe them all.

    This lad was known as Nicholas the Gallant,
And making love in secret was his talent,
For he was very close and sly, and took
Advantage of his meek and girlish look.
He rented a small chamber in the kip
All by himself without companionship.
He decked it charmingly with herbs and fruit
And he himself was sweeter than the root
Of liquorice, or any fragrant herb.
His astronomic text-books were superb,
He had an astrolabe to match his art
And calculating counters laid apart
On handy shelves that stood above his bed.
His press was curtained coarsely and in red;
Above there lay a gallant harp in sight
On which he played melodiously at night
With such a touch that all the chamber rang;
It was *The Virgin's Angelus* he sang,
And after that he sang *King William's Note*,
And people often blessed his merry throat.
And that was how this charming scholar spent
His time and money, which his friends had sent.

    This carpenter had married a new wife
Not long before, and loved her more than life.
She was a girl of eighteen years of age.
Jealous he was and kept her in the cage,
For he was old and she was wild and young;

He thought himself quite likely to be stung.

　　He might have known, were Cato on his shelf,
A man should marry someone like himself;
A man should pick an equal for his mate.
Youth and old age are often in debate.
However, he had fallen in the snare,
And had to bear his cross as others bear.

　　She was a fair young wife, her body as slender
As any weasel's, and as soft and tender;
She used to wear a girdle of striped silk;
Her apron was as white as morning milk
Over her loins, all gusseted and pleated.
White was her smock; embroidery repeated
Its pattern on the collar, front and back,
Inside and out; it was of silk, and black.
The tapes and ribbons of her milky mutch
Were made to match her collar to a touch;
She wore a broad silk fillet, rather high,
And certainly she had a lecherous eye.
And she had plucked her eyebrows into bows,
Slenderly arched they were, and black as sloes;
And a more truly blissful sight to see
She was than blossom on a cherry-tree,
And softer than the wool upon a wether;
And by her girdle hung a purse of leather,
Tasselled with silk and silver droplets, pearled;
If you went seeking up and down the world,
The wisest man you met would have to wrench
50 His fancy to imagine such a wench;

And her complexion had a brighter tint
Than new florin from the Royal Mint.
As to her song, it was as loud and quick
As any swallow's chirping on a rick;
And she would skip or play some game or other
Like any kid or calf behind its mother.
Her mouth was sweet as mead or honey—say
A hoard of apples lying in the hay.
Skittish she was, and jolly as a colt,
Tall as a mast and upright as a bolt
Out of a bow. Her collaret revealed
A brooch as big as boss upon a shield.
High shoes she wore, and laced them to the top.
She was a daisy, O a lollypop
For any nobleman to take to bed
Or some good man of yeoman stock to wed.

Now, gentlemen, this Gallant Nicholas
One day began to romp and make a pass
At this young woman, in a mood of play,
Her husband being out, down Osney way.
Students are sly, and giving way to whim,
He made a grab and caught her by the quim
And said, 'Unless I have my will of you
I'll die of secret love—O, darling, do!'
Then held her haunches hard and gave a cry
'O love-me-all-at-once or I shall die!'
She gave a spring, just like a skittish colt
Boxed in a frame for shoeing, and with a jolt
Managed in time to wrench her head away,

And said, 'Give over, Nicholas, I say!
No, I won't kiss you! Stop it! Let me go
Or I shall scream! I'll let the neighbours know!
Where are your manners? Take away your paws!'
      Then Nicholas began to plead his cause
And spoke so fair in proffering what he could
That in the end she promised him she would,
Swearing she'd love him, with a solemn promise
To be at his disposal, by St Thomas,
When she could spy an opportunity.
'My husband is so full of jealousy,
Unless you watch your step and hold your breath
I know for certain it will be my death,'
She said, 'So keep it well under your hat.'
'Oh, never mind about a thing like that.'
Said he; 'A scholar doesn't have to stir
His wits so much to trick a carpenter.'
      And so they both agreed to it, and swore
To watch their chance, as I have said before.
When things were settled thus as they thought fit,
And Nicholas had stroked her loins a bit
And kissed her sweetly, he took down his harp
And played away, a merry tune and sharp.
      It happened later she went off to church,
This worthy wife, one holiday, to search
Her conscience and to do the works of Christ.
She put her work aside and she enticed
The colour to her face to make her mark;
Her forehead shone. There was a parish clerk

Serving the church, whose name was Absalon.
His hair was all in golden curls and shone;
Just like a fan it strutted outwards, starting
To left and right from an accomplished parting.
Ruddy his face, his eyes as grey as goose,
His shoes cut out in tracery, as in use
In old St Paul's. The hose upon his feet
Showed scarlet through, and all his clothes were neat
And proper. In a jacket of light blue,
Flounced at the waist and tagged with laces too,
He went, and wore a surplice just as gay
And white as any blossom on the spray.
God bless my soul, he was a merry knave!
He knew how to let blood, cut hair and shave,
And draw up legal deed; at other whiles
He used to dance in twenty different styles
(After the current school at Oxford though,
Casting his legs about him to and fro).
He played a two-stringed fiddle, did it proud,
And sang a high falsetto, rather loud;
And he was just as good on the guitar.
There was no public-house in town, or bar,
He didn't visit with his merry face
If there were saucy barmaids round the place.
He was a little squeamish in the matter
Of farting, and satirical in chatter.
This Absalon, so jolly in his ways,
Would bear the censer round on holy days
And cense the parish women. He would cast

Many a love-lorn look before he passed,
Especially at this carpenter's young wife;
Looking at her would make a happy life
She was so neat, so sweet, so lecherous!
And I dare say if she had been a mouse
And he a cat, she'd have been pounced upon.

In taking the collection Absalon
Would find his heart was set in such a whirl
Of love, he would take nothing from a girl,
For courtesy, he said, it wasn't right.

That evening, when the moon was shining bright
He ups with his guitar and off he tours
On the look-out for any paramours.
Larky and amorous, away he strode
Until he reached the carpenter's abode
A little after cock-crow, took his stand
Beside the casement window close at hand
(It was set low upon the cottage-face)
And started singing softly and with grace,

   'Now dearest lady, if thy pleasure be
   In thoughts of love, think tenderly of me!'
On his guitar he plucked a tuneful string.

This carpenter awoke and heard him sing
And turning to his wife said, 'Alison!
Wife! Do you hear him? There goes Absalon
Chanting away under our chamber wall.'
And she, 'Yes, John, God knows I hear it all.'
If she thought more of it she didn't tell.
So things went on. What better than 'All's well'?

From day to day this jolly Absalon,
Wooing away, became quite woe-begone;
He lay awake all night, and all the day,
Combed his thick locks and tried to pass for gay,
Wooed her by go-between and wooed by proxy,
Swore to be page and servant to his doxy,
Trilled and rouladed like a nightingale,
Sent her sweet wine and mead and spicy ale,
And wagers piping hot and jars of honey,
And, as she lived in town, he offered money.
For there are some a money-bag provokes
And some are won by kindness, some by strokes.

Once, in the hope his talent might engage,
He played the part of Herod on the stage.
What was the good? Were he as bold as brass,
She was in love with gallant Nicholas:
However Absalon might blow his horn
His labour won him nothing but her scorn.
She looked upon him as her private ape
And held his earnest wooing all a jape.
There is a proverb, true, as you may find,
That *Out-of-Sight* is also *Out-of-Mind*.
For *Nigh-and-Sly* has the advantage there;
And, much as Absalon might tear his hair,
And rage at being seldom in her sight,
Nicholas, nigh and sly, stood in his light.
Now, show your paces, Nicholas you spark!
And leave lamenting to the parish clerk.

And so it happened that one Saturday,

When the old carpenter was safe away
At Osney, Nicholas and Alison
Agreed at last in what was to be done.
Nicholas was to exercise his wits
On her suspicious husband's foolish fits,
And, if so be the trick worked out all right,
She then would sleep with Nicholas all night,
For such was his desire and hers as well;
And even quicker than it takes to tell,
Young Nicholas, who simply couldn't wait,
Went to his room on tip-toe with a plate
Of food and drink, enough to last a day
Or two, and Alison was told to say,
In case her husband asked for Nicholas,
That she had no idea where he was,
And that she hadn't set eyes on him all day
And thought he must be ill, she couldn't say;
And more than once the maid had given a call
And shouted but no answer came at all.

So it continued, all that Saturday
Without a sound from Nicholas, who lay
Upstairs, and ate or slept as pleased him best
Till Sunday when the sun went down to rest.

This foolish carpenter was lost in wonder
At Nicholas; what could have got him under?
He said, 'I can't help thinking, by the Mass,
Things can't be going right with Nicholas.
What if he took and died? God guard his ways!
A ticklish place the world is, nowadays.

I saw a corpse this morning borne to kirk
That only Monday last I saw at work.
Run up,' he told the serving-lad, 'be quick,
Shout at his door, or knock it with a brick.
Take a good look and tell me how he fares.'
   The serving-boy went sturdily upstairs,
Stopped at the door and, standing there, the lad
Shouted away and, hammering like mad,
Cried, 'Ho! What's up? Hi! Master Nicholay!
How can you lie up there asleep all day?'
   But all for nought, he didn't hear a soul.
He found a broken panel with a hole
Right at the bottom, useful to the cat
For creeping in by: so he looked through that,
And, in the end, he saw him through the crack.
This Nicholas lay gaping on his back
As if he'd caught a glimpse of the new moon.
Down went the boy and told his master soon
About the state in which he found the man.
   On hearing this the carpenter began
To cross himself and said, 'St Frideswide bless us!
We little know what's coming to distress us.
The man has fallen, with this here 'astromy',
Into a fit, or lunacy maybe.
I always thought that was how it would go.
God has some secrets that we shouldn't know.
How blessed are the simple, aye, indeed,
That only know enough to say their creed!
Happened just so with such another student

57

Of astromy and he was so imprudent
As to stare upwards while he crossed a field,
Busy foreseeing what the stars revealed;
And what should happen but he fell down flat
Into a marl-pit. He didn't foresee that!
But by the Saints we've reached a sorry pass;
I can't help worrying for Nicholas.
He shall be scolded for his studying
If I know how to scold, by Christ the King!
Get me a staff to prise against the floor.
Robin, you put your shoulder to the door.
We'll shake the study out of him, I guess!'

  The pair of them began to heave and press
Against the door. Happened the lad was strong
And so it didn't take them very long
To heave it off its hinges; down it came.
Still as stone lay Nicholas, with the same
Expression, gaping upwards into air.
The carpenter supposed it was despair
And caught him by the shoulders mightily,
Shook him and shouted with asperity:
'What, Nicholas! Hey! Look down! Is that a fashion
To act? Wake up and think upon Christ's passion.
I sign you with the cross from elves and sprites!'
And he began the spell for use at nights
In all four corners of the room and out
Across the threshold too and round about:
  Jesu Christ and Benedict Sainted

  Bless this house from creature tainted,

> *Drive away night-hags, white Pater-noster,*
> *Where did you go, St Peter's soster?*

And in the end the dandy Nicholas
Began to sigh, 'And must it come to pass?'
He said, 'Must all the world be cast away?'
The carpenter replied, 'What's that you say?
Put trust in God as we do, working men.'
Nicholas answered, 'Fetch some liquor then,
And afterwards, in strictest secrecy,
I'll speak of something touching you and me,
But not another soul must know, that's plain.'

This carpenter went down and came again
Bringing some powerful ale—a largish quart.
When each had had his share of this support
Young Nicholas got up and shut the door
And, sitting down beside him on the floor,
Said to the carpenter, 'Now, John, my dear,
My excellent host, swear on your honour here
Not to repeat a syllable I say,
For here are Christ's intentions, to betray
Which to a soul puts you among the lost,
And vengeance for it at a bitter cost
Shall fall upon you. You'll be driven mad!'
'Christ and His holy blood forbid it, lad!'
The silly fellow answered. 'I'm no blab,
Though I should say it. I'm not given to gab.
Say what you like, for I shall never tell
Man, woman or child by Him that harrowed Hell!'

'Now, John,' said Nicholas, 'believe you me,

59

I have found out by my astrology,
And looking at the moon when it was bright,
That Monday next, a quarter way through night,
Rain is to fall in torrents, such a scud
It will be twice as bad as Noah's Flood.
This world,' he said, 'in just about an hour,
Shall all be drowned, it's such a hideous shower,
And all mankind, with total loss of life.'

    The carpenter exclaimed, 'Alas, my wife!
My little Alison! Is she to drown?'
And in his grief he very near fell down.
'Is there no remedy,' he said, 'for this?'
'Thanks be to God,' said Nicholas, 'there is,
If you will do exactly what I say
And don't start thinking up some other way.
In wise old Solomon you'll find the verse
"Who takes advice shall never fare the worse,"
And so if good advice is to prevail
I undertake with neither mast nor sail
To save her yet, and save myself and you.
Haven't you heard how Noah was saved too
When God forewarned him and his sons and daughters
That all the world should sink beneath the waters?'
'Yes,' said the carpenter, 'a long time back.'
'Haven't you heard,' said Nicholas, 'what a black
Business it was, when Noah tried to whip
His wife (who wouldn't come) on board the ship?
He'd have been better pleased, I'll undertake,
60 With all that weather just about to break,

If she had had a vessel of her own.
Now, what are we to do? We can't postpone
The thing; it's coming soon, as I was saying,
It calls for haste, not preaching or delaying.

  'I want you, now, at once, to hurry off
And fetch a shallow tub or kneading-trough
For each of us, but see that they are large
And such as we can float in, like a barge.
And have them loaded with sufficient victual
To last a day—we only need a little.
The waters will abate and flow away
Round nine o'clock upon the following day.
Robin the lad mayn't know of this, poor knave,
Nor Jill the maid, those two I cannot save.
Don't ask me why; and even if you do
I can't disclose God's secret thoughts to you.
You should be satisfied, unless you're mad,
To find as great a grace as Noah had.
And I shall save your wife, you needn't doubt it,
Now off you go, and hurry up about it.

  'And when the tubs have been collected, three,
That's one for her and for yourself and me,
Then hang them in the roof below the thatching
That no one may discover what we're hatching.
When you have finished doing what I said
And stowed the victuals in them overhead,
Also an axe to hack the ropes apart,
So, when the water rises, we can start,
And, lastly, when you've broken out the gable,

The garden one that's just above the stable,
So that we may cast free without delay
After the mighty shower has gone away,
You'll float as merrily, I undertake,
As any lily-white duck behind her drake.
And I'll call out, "Hey, Alison! Hey, John!
Cheer yourselves up! The flood will soon be gone."
And you'll shout back, "Hail, Master Nicholay!
Good morning! I can see you well. It's day!"
We shall be lords for all the rest of life
Of all the world, like Noah and his wife.

   'One thing I warn you of; it's only right.
We must be very careful on the night,
Once we have safely managed to embark,
To hold our tongues, to utter no remark,
No cry or call, for we must fall to prayer.
This is the Lord's dear will, so have a care.

   'Your wife and you must hang some way apart,
For there must be no sin before we start,
No more in longing looks than in the deed.
Those are your orders. Off with you! God speed!
To-morrow night when everyone's asleep
We'll all go quietly upstairs and creep
Into our tubs, awaiting Heaven's grace.
And now be off. No time to put the case
At greater length, no time to sermonize;
The proverb says, "Say nothing, send the wise.'
You're wise enough, I do not have to teach you.
Go, save our lives for us, as I beseech you.'

This silly carpenter then went his way
Muttering to himself, 'Alas the day!'
And told his wife in strictest secrecy.
She was aware, far more indeed than he,
What this quaint stratagem might have in sight,
But she pretended to be dead with fright.
'Alas!' she said. 'Whatever it may cost,
Hurry and help, or we shall all be lost.
I am your honest, true and wedded wife,
Go, dearest husband, help to save my life!'

How fancy throws us into perturbation!
People can die of mere imagination,
So deep is the impression one can take.
This silly carpenter began to quake,
Before his eyes there verily seemed to be
The flood of Noah, wallowing like the sea
And drowning Alison his honey-pet.
He wept and wailed, his features were all set
In grief, he sighed with many a doleful grunt.
He went and got a tub, began to hunt
For kneading-troughs, found two, and had them sent
Home to his house in secret; then he went
And, unbeknowns, he hung them from a rafter.
With his own hands he made three ladders after,
Uprights and rungs, to help them in their scheme
Of climbing where they hung upon the beam.
He victualled tub and trough, and made all snug
With bread and cheese, and ale in a large jug,
Enough for three of them to last the day,

And, just before completing this array,
Packed off the maid and his apprentice too
To London on a job they had to do.
And on the Monday when it drew to night
He shut his door and dowsed the candle-light
And made quite sure all was as it should be.
And shortly, up they clambered, all the three,
Silent and separate. They began to pray
And *'Pater Noster* mum', said Nicholay,
And 'mum' said John, and 'mum' said Alison.
The carpenter's devotions being done,
He sat quite still, then fell to prayer again
With one ear cocked, however, for the rain.

The carpenter, with all the work he'd seen,
Fell dead asleep—round curfew, must have been,
Maybe a little later on the whole.
He groaned in sleep for travail of his soul
And snored because his head was turned awry.

Down by their ladders, stalking from on high
Came Nicholas and Alison, and sped
Softly downstairs, without a word, to bed,
And where this carpenter was wont to be
The revels started and the melody.
And thus lay Nicholas and Alison
Busy in solace and the quest of fun,
Until the bell for lauds had started ringing
And in the chancel friars began their singing.

This parish clerk, this amorous Absalon,
Love-stricken still and very woe-begone,

Upon the Monday was in company
At Osney with his friends for jollity,
And chanced to ask a resident cloisterer
What had become of John the carpenter.
The fellow drew him out of church to say,
'Don't know; not been at work since Saturday.
I can't say where he is; I think he went
To fetch the Abbot timber. He is sent
Often enough for timber, has to go
Out to the Grange and stop a day or so;
If not, he's certainly at home to-day,
But where he is I can't exactly say.'
    Absalon was a jolly lad and light
Of heart; he thought, 'I'll stay awake to-night;
I'm certain that I haven't seen him stirring
About his door since dawn; it's safe inferring
That he's away. As I'm alive I'll go
And tap his window softly at the crow
Of cock—the sill is low-set in the wall.
I shall see Alison and tell her all
My love-longing, and I can hardly miss
Some favour from her, at the least a kiss.
I'll get some satisfaction anyway;
There's been an itching in my mouth all day
And that's a sign of kissing at the least.
And all last night I dreamt about a feast.
I think I'll go and sleep an hour or two,
Then wake and have some fun, that's what I'll do.'
    The first cock crew at last, and thereupon

Up rose this jolly lover Absalon
In gayest clothes, garnished with that and this;
But first he chewed a grain of liquorice
To charm his breath before he combed his hair.
Under his tongue the comfit nestling there
Would make him gracious. He began to roam
Towards the carpenter's; he reached their home
And by the casement window took his stand.
Breast-high it stood, no higher than his hand.
He gave a cough, it was a semi-sound;
'Alison, honey-comb, are you around?
Sweet cinnamon, my little pretty bird,
Sweetheart, wake up and say a little word!
You seldom think of me in all my woe,
I sweat for love of you wherever I go!
No wonder if I do, I pine and bleat
As any lambkin hungering for the teat,
Belive me, darling, I'm so deep in love
I croon with longing like a turtle-dove,
I eat as little as a girl at school.'
'You go away,' she answered, 'you Tom-fool!
There's no come-up-and-kiss-me here for you.
I love another and why shouldn't I too?
Better than you, by Jesu, Absalon!
Take yourself off or I shall throw a stone.
I want to get some sleep. You go to Hell!'
'Alas!' said Absalon. 'I knew it well;
True love is always mocked and girded at;
So kiss me, if you can't do more than that,

For Jesu's love and for the love of me!'
'And if I do, will you be off?' said she.
'Promise you, darling,' answered Absalon.
'Get ready then; wait, I'll put something on,'
She said and then she added under breath
To Nicholas, 'Hush . . . we shall laugh to death!'

This Absalon went down upon his knees;
'I am a lord!' he thought, 'And by degrees
There may be more to come; the plot may thicken.'
'Mercy, my love!' he said, 'Your mouth, my chicken!'

She flung the window open then in haste
And said, 'Have done, come on, no time to waste,
The neighbours here are always on the spy.'

Absalon started wiping his mouth dry.
Dark was the night as pitch, as black as coal,
And at the window out she put her hole,
And Absalon, so fortune framed the farce,
Put up his mouth and kissed her naked arse
Most savorously before he knew of this.

And back he started. Something was amiss;
He knew quite well a woman has no beard,
Yet something rough and hairy had appeared.
'What have I done?' he said. 'Can that be you?'
'Teehee!' she cried and clapped the window to.
Off went poor Absalon sadly through the dark.
'A beard! a beard!' cried Nicholas the Spark.
'God's body, that was something like a joke!'
And Absalon, overhearing what he spoke,
Bit on his lips and nearly threw a fit

In rage and thought, 'I'll pay you back for it!'
Who's busy rubbing, scraping at his lips
With dust, with sand, with straw, with cloth, with chips,
But Absalon? He thought 'I'll bring him down!
I wouldn't let this go for all the town.
I'd take my soul and sell it to the Devil.
To be revenged upon him! I'll get level.
O God, why did I let myself be fooled?'
The fiery heat of love by now had cooled,
For from the time he kissed her hinder parts
He didn't give a tinker's curse for tarts;
His malady was cured by this endeavour
And he defied all paramours whatever.

So, weeping like a child that has been whipped,
He turned away; across the road he slipped
And called on Gervase. Gervase was a smith;
His forge was full of things for ploughing with
And he was busy sharpening a share.
Absalon knocked, and with an easy air
Called, 'Gervase! Open up the door, come on!'
'What's that? Who's there?' 'It's me, it's Absalon.'
'What, Absalon? By Jesu's blessed tree
You're early up! Hey, *benedicite*,
What's wrong? Some jolly girl as like as not
Has coaxed you out and set you on the trot.
Blessed St Neot! You know the thing I mean.'
But Absalon, who didn't give a bean
For all his joking, offered no debate.
He had a good deal more upon his plate

Than Gervase knew and said, 'Would it be fair
To borrow that coulter in the chimney there,
The hot one, see it? I've a job to do;
It won't take long, I'll bring it back to you.'
Gervase replied, 'Why, if you asked for gold,
A bag of sovereigns or of wealth untold,
It should be yours, as I'm an honest smith.
But, Christ, why borrow that to do it with?'
'Let that,' said Absalon, 'be as it may;
You'll hear about it all some other day.'

He caught the coulter up—the haft was cool—
And left the smithy softly with the tool,
Crept to the little window in the wall
And coughed. He knocked and gave a little call
Under the window as he had before.

Alison said, 'There's someone at the door.
Who's knocking there? I'll warrant it's a thief.'
'Why, no,' said he, 'my little flower-leaf,
It's your own Absalon, my sweety-thing!
Look what I've brought you—it's a golden ring
My mother gave me, as I may be saved.
It's very fine, and prettily engraved;
I'll give it to you, darling, for a kiss.'

Now Nicholas had risen for a piss,
And thought he could improve upon the jape
And make him kiss his arse ere he escape,
And opening the window with a jerk,
Stuck out his arse, a handsome piece of work,
Buttocks and all, as far as to the haunch.

69

Said Absalon, all set to make a launch,
'Speak, pretty bird, I know not where thou art!'
This Nicholas at once let fly a fart
As loud as if it were a thunder-clap.
He was near blinded by the blast, poor chap,
But his hot iron was ready; with a thump
He smote him in the middle of the rump.

Off went the skin a hand's breadth round about
Where the hot coulter struck and burnt it out.
Such was the pain, he thought he must be dying
And, mad with agony, he started crying,
'Help! Water! Water! Help! For Heaven's love!'

The carpenter, startled from sleep above,
And hearing shouts for water and a thud,
Thought, 'Heaven help us! Here comes Nowel's Flood!'
And up he sat and with no more ado
He took his axe and smote the ropes in two
And down went everything. He didn't stop
To sell his bread and ale, but came down flop
Upon the floor and fainted right away.

Up started Alison and Nicholay
And shouted, 'Help!' and 'Murder!' in the street.
The neighbours all came running up in heat
And stood there staring at the wretched man.
He lay there fainting, pale beneath his tan;
His arm in falling had been broken double.
Bit still he was obliged to face his trouble,
For when he spoke he was at once borne down
By Nicholas and his wife. They told the town

That he was mad, there'd got into his blood
Some sort of nonsense about 'Nowel's Flood',
That vain imaginings and fantasy
Had made him buy the kneading-tubs, that he
Had hung them in the rafters up above
And that he'd begged them both for heaven's love
To sit up in the roof for company.
   All started laughing at this lunacy
And streamed upstairs to gape and pry and poke,
And treated all his sufferings as a joke.
No matter what the carpenter asserted
It went for nothing, no one was converted;
With powerful oaths they swore the fellow down
And he was held for mad by all the town;
The students all ganged up with one another
Saying: 'The fellow's crazy, my dear brother!'
And every one among them laughed and joked.
And so the carpenter's wife was truly poked,
As if his jealousy to justify,
And Absalon has kissed her nether eye
And Nicholas is branded on the bum
And God bring all of us to Kingdom Come.

THE REEVE'S TALE

The Reeve's Prologue

When all had laughed at the preposterous lark
of Absalon and Nicholas the Spark,
Various folk made various comment after;
But the majority dissolved in laughter,
Nor did I see a soul it seemed to grieve
Unless it might be Oswald, the old Reeve,
For, as he was a carpenter by trade,
He was a little angry still and made
Grumbling remarks and scolded for a bit.
  'As I'm a man I'd pay you back for it,'
He said, 'with how they bleared a Miller's eye,
If I liked dirt and wished to argufy.
But I am old. Dirt doesn't go with doddering,
Grass-time is done and I'm for winter foddering.
My hoary top-knot writes me down for old;
Same as my hair, my heart is full of mould,
Unless I be like them there medlar-fruit,
Them that gets rottener as they ripen to't,
Till they be rotted down in straw and dung.
That's how we get to be, no longer young.

Till we be rotten we can never ripe.

We hop along, as long as world will pipe;
Our will is always catching on the nail,
Wanting a hoary head and a green tail,
Like leeks have got; the strength to play that game
Is gone, though we love foolishness the same.
What we can't do no more we talk about
And rake the ashes when the fire is out.

'Yet we have four live coals, as I can show;
Lies, boasting, greed and rage will always glow.
Those are the sparks among the ancient embers
Though we be nigh unwelded in our members.
Desire never fails, and that's the truth,
For even now I have a coltish tooth,
Many as be the years now dead and done
Before my tap of life began to run.
Certain, when I was born, so long ago,
Death drew the tap of life and let it flow;
And ever since the tap has done its task,
And now there's little but an empty cask.
My stream of life's but drops upon the rim.
An old fool's tongue will run away with him
To chime and chatter of monkey-tricks that's past;
There's nothing left but dotage at the last!'

Our Host, on hearing all this sermoning,
Began to speak as lordly as a king,
And said, 'What does it come to, all this wit?
What! Spend the morning talking Holy Writ?
The devil that makes a preacher of a Reeve
Turns cobblers into doctors, I believe.

Give us your story, if you've one in stock.
Why, look! Here's Deptford and it's nine o'clock!
And Greenwich too, with many a blackguard in it.
High time to tell your story, so begin it.'

  'Now, gentlemen,' Oswald the Reeve replied,
'I hope as none will be dissatisfied
Though I should tweak the Miller by the cap,
For lawful 'tis to give him tap for tap.

  'This drunken Miller we've had so much drool of,
Told how a carpenter was made a fool of,
Maybe to score off me, for I am one.
By y'r leave, I'll pay him back before I've done
In his own filthy words, you may expec'.
I hope to God he breaks his bloody neck.
He sees the mote in my eye, if there is un,
But cannot see the beam there is in his'n.'

The Reeve's Tale

At Trumpington, not far from Cambridge town,
A bridge goes over where the brook runs down
And by that brook there stands a mill as well.
And it's God's truth that I am going to tell.

  There was a miller lived there many a day
As proud as any peacock and as gay;
He could play bag-pipes too, fish, mend his gear,
And turn a lathe, and wrestle, and poach deer.

74 And at his belt he carried a long blade,

Trenchant it was as any sword that's made,
And in his pouch a jolly little knife.
No one dared touch him, peril of his life.
He had a Sheffield dagger in his hose.
Round was his face and puggish was his nose;
Bald as an ape he was. To speak more fully,
He was a thorough-going market bully
Whom none dared lay a hand on or come near
Without him swearing that they'd buy it dear.

He was a thief as well of corn and meal,
And sly at that; his habit was to steal.
Simpkin the Swagger he was called in scorn.
He had a wife and she was nobly born;
Her father was the parson of the town;
A dowry of brass dishes he put down
In order to have Simpkin his relation.
The nuns had given her an education.
Simpkin would take no woman, so he said,
Unless she were a virgin and well-bred,
To save the honour of his yeoman stock;
And she was proud, pert as a magpie cock.

It was a proper sight to see the pair
On holidays, what with him strutting there
In front of her, his hood about his head,
And she behind him all decked out in red,
Like Simpkin's hose, for scarlet-red he had 'em.
No one dared call her anything but 'Madam',
No one who passed was bold enough to try
A bit of fun with her or wink an eye,

Unless indeed he wanted Sim the Swagger
To murder him with cutlass, knife or dagger,
For jealous folk are dangerous, you know,
At least they want their wives to think them so.
And then her birth was smirched to say the least;
Being the daughter of a celibate priest
She must maintain her dignity, of which
She had as much as water in a ditch.
She was a sneering woman and she thought
That ladies should respect her, so they ought,
What with her well-connected family,
And education in a nunnery.

They had a daughter too between them both,
She was a girl of twenty summers' growth;
But that was all except a child they had
Still in the cradle, but a proper lad.
The wench was plump, well-grown enough to pass,
With a snub nose and eyes as grey as glass;
Her rump was broad, her breasts were round and high;
She'd very pretty hair, I will not lie.
The parson of the town, for she was fair,
Intended to appoint the girl as heir
To all his property in house and land
And he was stiff with suitors to her hand.
He purposed to bestow her if he could
Where blood and ancient lineage made it good.
For Holy Church's goods should be expended
On Holy Church's blood, so well-descended,

And holy blood should have what's proper to it

Though Holy Church should be devoured to do it.

   This miller levied toll beyond a doubt
On wheat and malt from all the land about,
Particularly from a large-sized College
In Cambridge, Solar Hall. 'Twas common knowledge
They sent their wheat and malt to him to grind it.
Happened one day the man who ought to mind it,
The college manciple, lay sick in bed,
And some reported him as good as dead.
On hearing which the miller robbed him more
A hundred times than he had robbed before;
For up till then he'd only robbed politely,
But now he stole outrageously, forthrightly.

   The Warden scolded hard and made a scene,
But there! The miller didn't give a bean,
Blustered it out and swore it wasn't so.

   Two poor young Bible-clerks or students, though,
Lived in this College (that of which I spoke).
Headstrong they were and eager for a joke,
And simply for the chance of sport and play
They went and plagued the Warden night and day
Just for a little leave to spend the morn
Watching the miller grind their meal and corn,
And each was ready to engage his neck
The miller couldn't rob them half a peck
Of corn by trickery, nor yet by force;
And in the end he gave them leave, of course.

   One was called John and Alan was the other,
Both born in the same village, name of Strother,

Far in the north, I cannot tell you where.
    Alan collected all his gear with care,
Loaded it on a horse the warden had,
And off he went with John the other lad,
Each with his sword and buckler by his side.
John knew the way—he didn't need a guide—
Reaches the mill and down the sack he flings.
    Alan spoke first: 'Well, Simon, lad, how's things?
And how's your canny daughter and your wife?'
Says Simpkin, 'Welcome, Alan! Odds my life,
It's John as well! What, are you in the sequel?'
'By God,' said John, 'Needs-must has got no equal,
And it behoves a man that has nie servant
To work, as say the learned and observant.
Wor Manciple is like enough to dee,
Such aches and torments in his teeth has he;
So Alan here and I have brought wor sack
Of corn for grinding and to bring it back.
Help us get home as quickly as ye can.'
'It shall be done,' said he, 'as I'm a man.
What'll you do while I've the job in hand?'
'By God,' said John, 'I have a mind to stand
Right by the hopper here and watch the corn
As it gans in. Never since I was born
Saw I a hopper wagging to and fro.'
    Alan spoke up: 'Eh, John, and will ye so?
Then I shall stand below a short way off
And watch the meal come down into the trough;
78 I need no more than that by way of sport,

For John, in faith, I'm one of the same sort
And diven't knaa nowt of milling, same as ye.'
    The miller smiled at their simplicity
And thought, 'It's just a trick, what they're about,
They think that nobody can catch them out,
But by the Lord I'll blear their eyes a bit
For all their fine philosophy and wit.
The more they try to do me on the deal,
When the time comes, the more I mean to steal.
Instead of flour I will give them bran;
"The greatest scholar is not the wisest man",
As the wolf said in answer to the mare.
Them and their precious learning! Much I care.'
    And when he saw his chance he sidled out
Into the yard behind and looked about
Without their noticing until at last
He found their horse where they had made him fast
Under an arbour just behind the mill.
    Up to the horse he goes with quiet skill
And strips the bridle off him there and then.
And when the horse was loose, off to the fen
Through thick and thin, and whinneying 'Weehee!'
He raced to join the wild mares running free.
    The miller then went back, and did not say
A word of this, but passed the time of day
With John and Alan till their corn was ground;
And when the meal was fairly sacked and bound,
John wandered out and found their horse was gone.
'Good Lord! Help! Help! Come quickly!' shouted John,   79

'Wor horse is lost, Alan! The devil's in it!
God's bones, man, use your legs! Come out this minute!
Lord save us all, the Warden's palfrey's lost.'

    Alan forgot his meal and corn and cost,
Abandoning frugality and care.
'What's that?' he shouted. 'Palfrey? Which way? Where?'

    The miller's wife ran clucking like a hen
Towards them, saying, 'Gone off to the fen
To the wild mares as fast as he can go.
Curse on the clumsy hand that tied him so!
Should have known better how to knit the reins.'
John said, 'Bad luck to it. Alan, for Christ's pains,
Put down your sword, man; so will I; let's gan!
We'll rin him like a roe together, man!
God's precious heart! He cannot scape us all!
Why didn't you put the palfrey in the stall?
You must be daft, bad luck to you! Haway!'
And off ran John and Alan in dismay,
Towards the fen as fast as they could go.

    And when the miller saw that this was so,
A good half-bushel of their flour he took
And gave it over to his wife to cook.
'I think,' he said, 'these lads have had a fright.
I'll pluck their beards. Yes, let 'em read and write,
But none the less a miller is their match.
Look at them now! Like children playing catch.
Won't be an easy job to get him, though!'

    These foolish Bible-clerks ran to and fro
80 And shouted, 'Woa, lad, stand! . . . Look out behind!

Whistle him up . . . I've got him . . . watch it . . . *mind!*'
But to be brief, it wasn't until night
They caught the palfrey, hunt him as they might
Over the fens, he ran away so fast;
But in a ditch they captured him at last.

Weary and wet, like cattle in the rain,
Came foolish John and Alan back again.
Said John, 'Alas the day that I was born!
We've earned nowt here but mockery and scorn.
Wor corn is stolen and they'll call us fools,
Warden and all wor meäts in the Schools,
And most of all the miller. What a day!'

So back they went, John grousing all the way,
Towards the mill and put the horse in byre.
They found the miller sitting by the fire,
For it was night, too late for going home,
And, for the love of God, they begged a room
For shelter and they proffered him their penny.
'A room?' the miller said. 'There isn't any.
There's this, such as it is; we'll share it then.
My house is small, but you are learned men
And by your arguments can make a place
Twenty foot broad as infinite as space.
Take a look round and see if it will do,
Or make it bigger with your parley-voo.'
'Well, Simon, you must have your little joke
And, by St Cuthbert, that was fairly spoke!
Well, people have a proverb to remind them
To bring their own, or take things as they find them,'   81

Said John, 'Dear host, do get us out the cup;
A little meat and drink would cheer us up.
We'll give ye the full payment, on my word.
No empty-handed man can catch a bird;
See, here's the silver, ready to be spent.'

   Down into Trumpington the daughter went
For bread and ale; the miller cooked a goose,
And tied their horse up lest it should get loose
Again, and in his chamber made a bed
With clean white sheets and blankets fairly spread,
Ten foot from his, upon a sort of shelf.
His daughter had a bed all by herself
Quite close in the same room; they were to lie
All side by side, no help for it, and why?
Because there was no other in the house.

   They supped and talked and had a fine carouse
And drank a lot of ale, the very best.
Midnight or thereabout they went to rest.

   Properly pasted was this miller's head,
Pale-drunk he was, he'd passed the stage of red;
Hiccupping through his nose he talked and trolled
As if he'd asthma or a heavy cold.
To bed he goes, his wife and he together;
She was as jolly as a jay in feather,
Having well wet her whistle from the ladle.
And by her bed she planted down the cradle
To rock the baby or give it sup.

   When what was in the crock had been drunk up,
To bed went daughter too, and thereupon

To bed went Alan and to bed went John.
That was the lot; no sleeping-draught was needed.
The miller had taken so much booze unheeded,
He snorted like a cart-horse in his sleep
And vented other noises, loud and deep.
His wife joined in the chorus hot and strong;
Two furlongs off you might have heard their song.
The wench was snoring too, for company.
   Alan the clerk in all this melody
Gave John a poke and said, 'Are ye awake?
Did ye ever hear sich sang for guidness sake?
There's family prayers for ye among they noddies!
Wild fire come doon and burn them up, the bodies!
Who ever heard a canny thing like that?
The devil take their souls for what they're at!
All this lang neet I shall na get nie rest.
   'But never ye mind, all shall be for the best;
I tell ye, John, as sure as I'm a man,
I'm going to have that wench there, if I can!
The law grants easement when things gan amiss,
For, John, there is a law that gans like this:
"If in one point a person be aggrieved,
Then in another he shall be relieved."
   'Wor corn is stolen, nivvor doubt of that;
Ill-luck has followed us in all we're at,
And since no compensation has been offered
Against wor loss, I'll take the easement proffered.
God's soul, it shall be so indeed, none other!'
   John whispered back to him, 'Be careful, brother,

The miller is a torble man for slaughter;
If he should wake and find ye with his daughter
He might do injury to you and me.'
'Injury? Him! I coont him nat a flea!'

Alan rose up; towards the wench he crept.
The wench lay flat upon her back and slept,
And ere she saw him, he had drawn so nigh
It was too late for her to give a cry.
To put it briefly, they were soon at one.
Now, Alan, play! For I will speak of John.

John lay there still for quite a little while,
Complaining and lamenting in this style:
'A bloody joke . . . Lord, what a chance to miss!
I shall be made a monkey of for this!
My meät has got some comfort for his harms,
He has the miller's daughter in his arms;
He took his chance and now his needs are sped,
I'm but a sack of rubbish here in bed.
And when this jape is told in time to come
They'll say I was a softie and a bum!
I'll get up too and take what chance I may,
For God helps those that help theirsels, they say.'

He rises, steals towards the cradle, lifts it,
And stepping softly back again, he shifts it
And lays it by his bed upon the floor.

The miller's wife soon after ceased to snore,
Began to wake, rose up, and left the room,
And coming back she groped about in gloom,
84 Missing the cradle John had snatched away.

'Lord, Lord,' she said, 'I nearly went astray
And got into the student's bed . . . How dreadful!
There would have been foul doings. What a bed-ful!'
   At last she gropes to where the cradle stands,
And so by fumbling upwards with her hands
She found the bed and thinking nought but good.
Since she was certain where the cradle stood,
Yet knew not where she was, for it was dark,
She well and fairly crept in with the clerk,
Then lay quite still and tried to go to sleep.
John waited for a while, then gave a leap
And thrust himself upon this worthy wife.
It was the merriest fit in all her life,
For John went deep and thrust away like mad.
It was a jolly life for either lad
Till the third morning cock began to sing.
   Alan grew tired as dawn began to spring;
He had been hard at work the long, long night.
'Bye-bye,' he said, 'sweet Molly. . . . Are ye a'right?
The day has come, I cannot linger here,
But ever mair in life and death, my dear,
I am your own true clerk, or strike me deid!'
'Good-bye, my sweet,' she whispered, 'take good heed . . .
But first I'll tell you something, that I will!
When you are riding homewards past the mill
By the main entrance-door, a bit behind it,
There's the half-bushel cake—you're sure to find it—
And it was made out of the very meal
You brought to grind and I helped father steal. . . .

And, dearest heart, God have you in his keeping!'
And with that word she almost burst out weeping.

    Alan got up and thought, 'Dawn's coming on.
Better get back and creep in beside John.'
But there he found the cradle in his way.
'By God,' he thought, 'I nearly went astray!
My heid is tottering with my work to-neet,
That'll be why I cannot gan areet!
This cradle tells me I have lost my tether;
Yon must be miller and his wife together.'

    And back he went, groping his weary way
And reached the bed in which the miller lay,
And thinking it was John upon the bed
He slid in by the miller's side instead,
Grabbing his neck, and with no more ado
Said, 'Shake yourself, wake up, you pig's-head, you!
For Christ's soul, listen! O such noble games
As I have had! I tell you, by St James,
Three times the neet, from midnight into morn,
The miller's daughter helped me grind my corn
While you've been lying in your cowardly way . . .'
'You scoundrel!' said the miller. 'What d'you say?
You beast! You treacherous blackguard! Filthy rat!
God's dignity! I'll murder you for that!
How dare you be so bold as to fling mud
Upon my daughter, come of noble blood?'

    He grabbed at Alan by his Adam's apple,
And Alan grabbed him back in furious grapple
86 And clenched his fist and bashed him on the nose.

Down miller's breast a bloody river flows
Onto the floor, his nose and mouth all broke;
They wallowed like two porkers in a poke,
And up and down and up again they go
Until the miller tripped and stubbed his toe,
Spun round and fell down backwards on his wife.
　She had heard nothing of this foolish strife,
For she had fallen asleep with John the clerk,
Weary from all their labours in the dark.
The miller's fall started her out of sleep.
'Help! she screamed. 'Holy cross of Bromeholme keep
Us! Lord! Into thy hands! To Thee I call!
Simon, wake up! The devil's among us all!
My heart is bursting, help! I'm nearly dead,
One's on my belly, and another's in my head.
Help, Simpkin, help! These nasty clerks are fighting!'
　Up started John, he needed no inciting,
And groped about the chamber to and fro
To find a stick; she too was on the go
And, knowing the corners better than them all,
Was first to find one leaning by the wall;
And by a little shaft of shimmering light
That shone in through a hole—the moon was bright—
Although the room was almost black as pitch
She saw them fight, not knowing which was which;
But there was something white that caught her eye
On seeing which she peered and gave a cry,
Thinking it was the night-cap of the clerk.
　Raising her stick, she crept up in the dark

And, hoping to hit Alan, it was her fate
To smite the miller on his shining pate,
And down he went, shouting, 'O God, I'm dying!'

The clerks then beat him well and left him lying
And throwing on their clothes they took their horse
And their ground meal and off they went, of course,
And as they passed the mill they took the cake
Made of their meal the girl was told to bake.

And thus the bumptious miller was well beaten
And done out of the supper they had eaten,
And done out of the money that was due
For grinding Alan's corn, who beat him too.
His wife was plumbed, so was his daughter. Look!
That comes of being a miller and a crook!

I heard this proverb when I was a kid,
'Do evil and be done by as you did.'
Tricksters will get a tricking, so say I;
And God that sits in majesty on high
Bring all this company, great and small, to Glory!
Thus I've paid out the Miller with my story!

FOR THE BEST IN PAPERBACKS, LOOK FOR THE Ⓟ

In every corner of the world, on every subject under the sun, Penguin represents quality and variety—the very best in publishing today.

For complete information about books available from Penguin—including Puffins, Penguin Classics, and Arkana—and how to order them, write to us at the appropriate address below. Please note that for copyright reasons the selection of books varies from country to country.

In the United States: Please write to *Consumer Sales, Penguin USA, P.O. Box 999, Dept. 17109, Bergenfield, New Jersey 07621-0120.* VISA and MasterCard holders call 1-800-253-6476 to order all Penguin titles.

In Canada: Please write to *Penguin Books Canada Ltd, 10 Alcorn Avenue, Suite 300, Toronto, Ontario M4V 3B2.*

In the United Kingdom: Please write to *Dept. JC, Penguin Books Ltd, FREEPOST, West Drayton, Middlesex UB7 0BR.*